ULTIMATE STICKER BOOK
YODA'S JEDI ARMY

LONDON, NEW YORK,
MELBOURNE, MUNICH AND DELHI

Written by Shari Last
Edited by Garima Sharma
Designed by Lauren Rosier and Suzena Sengupta
Jacket designed by Suzena Sengupta
DTP Designer Umesh Singh Rawat

First published in Great Britain in 2014
by Dorling Kindersley Limited
80 Strand, London WC2R 0RL

10 9 8 7 6 5 4 3 2 1
001–257111–May/14

Page design copyright © 2014 Dorling Kindersley Limited
A Penguin Random House Company

A CIP catalogue record for this book is available from the British Library.

ISBN: 978-1-40935-364-5

Colour reproduction by Alta Image, UK
Printed and bound by
L-Rex Printing Co., Ltd, China

Discover more at
www.dk.com
www.LEGO.com
www.starwars.com

How to use this book

Read the captions, then find the
sticker that best fits the space.
(Hint: check the sticker labels for clues!)

•

Don't forget that your stickers can be
stuck down and peeled off again.

•

There are lots of fantastic extra
stickers for creating your own
scenes throughout the book.

TWO SIDES OF THE FORCE

The galaxy is in crisis. The peaceful Republic is under threat from corrupt Separatists, who do not want to live under Republic rule. The noble Jedi use the light side of the Force to defend the Republic. But the evil Sith have chosen the dangerous dark side of the Force – and they want to take control of the galaxy forever.

THE JEDI

The Jedi are powerful warriors who use the light side of the Force. They long for peace, but are prepared to battle against evil.

©2014 LEGO

PALPATINE

Chancellor Palpatine is the leader of the Republic. He pretends to want a peaceful galaxy, but he hides a very dark secret...

©2014 LEGO

DARTH MAUL

Darth Maul is a Sith. His body was cut in half by Jedi Obi-Wan Kenobi, so he walks on robotic legs. Now, Maul wants revenge!

COUNT DOOKU

Count Dooku used to be a Jedi, but he has turned to the dark side. Now, he leads the Separatists and commands the droid army.

©2014 LEGO

DARTH SIDIOUS

The evil Sith study the dark side of the Force. Darth Sidious is the Sith leader, but nobody knows he is Chancellor Palpatine in disguise.

©2014 LEGO

©2014 LEGO

GALAXY PATROL

This police gunship patrols the busy planet Coruscant – the capital of the Republic.

APPRENTICES

Count Dooku trained Asajj Ventress and Savage Opress as his Sith apprentices. But will these dangerous creatures ever truly obey him?

JEK-14

Jek-14 is created by Count Dooku to be the most powerful Sith apprentice ever. But Jek-14 is not sure if he wants to be evil...

JEDI OR SITH?

Jedi Anakin Skywalker is not able to resist the power of the dark side. He will soon turn against the Jedi and battle Obi-Wan Kenobi.

RISE OF A SITH LORD

When Anakin is injured during his battle with Obi-Wan, he becomes Darth Vader – an evil Sith Lord kept alive by a mechanical suit and mask.

BATTLE OF NABOO

The evil Sith Lord Darth Sidious wants to control the galaxy. He secretly organises an attack on the peaceful planet Naboo. On his orders, a massive droid army descends on the planet's grassy plains. The Gungan people of Naboo must decide whether to stand up and fight, or to surrender. Can they save their planet?

BATTLE DROID
Battle droids are controlled by the Separatists. They obey orders without question, but they cannot think for themselves.

©2014 LEGO

MTT
There are thousands of battle droids in the Separatist droid army. How will they get to the battlefield? Easy – each Multi-Troop Transport (MTT) can carry 112 battle droids!

JAR JAR BINKS
Jar Jar is a clumsy Gungan – but he really wants to help defend his home planet. During the battle, Jar Jar destroys lots of battle droids.

AAT
The Armoured Assault Tank (AAT) is a fearsome weapon. The droid army uses it to blast through everything in its way.

©2014 LEGO

NABOO STARFIGHTER
Up in space, hundreds of yellow Naboo starfighters attack droid control ships. Can they defeat the droid army?

Use your extra stickers to create your own scene.

READY FOR BATTLE

The droid army expects to conquer Naboo with ease – but they are in for a surprise!

BATTLE OF GEONOSIS

The Separatists have built a secret battle droid factory on the planet Geonosis. When the Jedi find out, they lead the Republic army of clone troopers in an attack on the growing Separatist army. On the desert plains of Geonosis, the Clone Wars have begun!

CLONE TROOPER

The Jedi build an army of clones to help them take on the droid army. The clone troopers fight without fear.

COMMAND STATION

The clone command station is well equipped to help clone sergeants direct their troops straight from the battlefield.

AT-TE

The All Terrain Tactical Enforcer (AT-TE) is an enormous walking tank. It can carry 38 clone troopers onto a battlefield.

ALLIANCE TANK DROID

This dangerous droid can roll over any terrain, flattening everything in its path. Clone troopers – watch out!

BARC SPEEDER

Obi-Wan Kenobi chases battle droids in the superfast BARC speeder. Its sidecar can rotate to fire the blaster cannon in all directions!

DROIDEKA

The droideka is designed to destroy clone troopers. It has twin blasters and a powerful defence shield.

AT-RT

The powerful All Terrain Reconnaissance Transport (AT-RT) has a swivelling laser cannon to blast any battle droids who get in its way.

HOMING SPIDER DROID

The spider droid can blast its laser weapon at targets on the ground and in the air. It can even walk underwater and climb walls!

COMMANDO DROID CAPTAIN

Commando droid captains are built to be faster, stronger and more intelligent than regular battle droids.

ARTILLERY CANNON

The clone army uses the artillery cannon to blast battle droids out of the way!

JEDI AT WAR

The Jedi are peacekeepers and prefer to avoid fighting, but they understand that sometimes there is no other option. During the Clone Wars, the brave Jedi swoop into battle aboard enormous Republic attack gunships. Enemies, beware!

SWOOP BIKE
Clone troopers use speedy swoop bikes to zip in and out of big battles.

OBI-WAN KENOBI
Obi-Wan keeps his cool in battle situations. He hates flying, but he happens to be an excellent pilot!

CLONE CAPTAIN
The clone trooper captain flies the Republic gunship. His ship can carry up to 30 clones.

COLEMAN TREBOR
Coleman is a Vurk, from the planet Sembla. He prefers negotiating to fighting, but is ready to wage war if he must.

SAESEE TIIN
Saesee Tiin has the ability to read minds. He uses this skill to his advantage in battles.

©2014 LEGO

ATTACK!
Republic gunships deploy troops into battle swiftly and safely.

NAVIGATION
Clone troopers are trained to navigate big starships and communicate with mission command.

ANAKIN SKYWALKER
Anakin has an excellent aim. He takes charge of the gun turrets – ready to shoot any Separatist battle droids he sees!

AGEN KOLAR
Like all Zabraks, Agen Kolar is fierce and strong. He is a faithful Jedi Master and is ready to defend the galaxy.

PADMÉ
Padmé Amidala is a senator, but she fights alongside the Jedi. She uses a blaster pistol to fire at the enemy Separatist forces.

9

BATTLE OF CORUSCANT

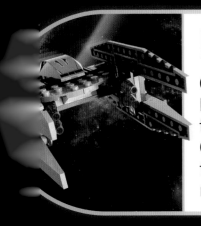

Chancellor Palpatine has been kidnapped! Obi-Wan Kenobi and Anakin Skywalker track him down aboard the starship of a droid army commander called General Grievous. As the Jedi fly through space above the planet Coruscant to rescue Palpatine, a huge battle rages between the Republic and Separatist fleets.

REPUBLIC ATTACK CRUISER

This huge ship carries hundreds of Republic starfighters into battle. It is also equipped with laser cannons and torpedo launchers.

©2014 LEGO

VULTURE DROID

Vulture droids fly through space without a pilot. They receive commands from a droid control ship and attack the Republic fleet.

DROID TRI-FIGHTE

The extremely fast and accurate droid tri-fighte fly unpiloted, too. These droids strike fear in the hearts of Republic pilot

V-WING PILO

V-wing pilots tra hard to fly their starfighters. The work together w an astromech d to avoid enemy

V-WING

The Republic V-wing starfighters are small and speedy. They can manoeuvre across a dangerous battlefield – and even escape droid tri-fighters!

ASTROMECH DROID

Small astromech droids help pilots with navigation and repair. They plug into special holes on top of starships.

PILOT ANAKIN

Anakin is a skilled Jedi pilot. He has amazing reflexes, which allow him to fly his starship at incredible speeds.

©2014 LEGO

BUZZ DROIDS ATTACK!

Buzz droids have latched on to Obi-Wan's Interceptor. Can the brave Jedi shake them off?

JEDI INTERCEPTOR

Anakin flies his yellow Jedi Interceptor towards Grievous's starship. The starfighter dodges attacks from approaching vulture droids.

BUZZ DROID

Oh no – swarms of buzz droids attack the Republic starships! These small, deadly droids destroy a starship's wiring.

©2014 LEGO

ROCKET BATTLE DROID

Rocket battle droids wear jetpacks and have floodlights so they can spot their enemies in space. Look out!

BATTLE OF KASHYYYK

When the Separatists invade the planet Kashyyyk with their vast droid army, the clone troopers are worried. But the battle turns quickly when the native Wookiees decide to fight for their planet. Thanks to the Jedi's smart planning and Wookiees' brute strength, it seems that victory is within reach for the Republic.

CHIEF TARFFUL

Tarfful is the chief of a tribe of Wookiees. He is not a general, but he leads the Wookiee army to protect his home planet.

JEDI GENERALS

Jedi Generals Quinlan Vos and Luminara Unduli lead the clone troopers on Kashyyyk. They fight alongside the Wookiee army.

CATAMARAN

The Wookiees have many vehicles for travelling across their swampy planet. The catamaran is a fast, sturdy boat, which can also fly in the air!

CHEWBACCA

Chewbacca is a brave soldier in the Wookiee army. He uses a powerful bowcaster to fire at the battle droids.

SUPER BATTLE DROID

These tall, scary droids are programmed to be fearless in battle. They shoot at their enemies with blasters built into their arms!

41ST ELITE TROOPER

Clone troopers from the 41st Elite Corps wear camouflage armour and masks to stay hidden in the swamps of Kashyyyk.

DROID GUNSHIP

This flying droid machine hovers above the battlefield, raining down blasts onto the Wookiees and clone troopers below.

OCEAN ATTACK

Separatist tanks swarm out of the oceans of Kashyyyk, catching the Wookiees by surprise!

COMMANDER GREE

Commander Gree leads the 41st Elite Corps. He is a loyal soldier and will do anything to help the Republic.

AT-AP

The Republic's All Terrain Attack Pod (AT-AP) is a walker with serious firepower. It can destroy many battle droids with just one shot.

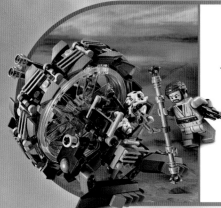

BATTLE OF UTAPAU

The droid army has taken over the planet Utapau. General Grievous is plotting with the Separatist council, preparing to make his next move. Obi-Wan Kenobi soon arrives and confronts Grievous in a fierce lightsaber duel. Meanwhile, the Republic army launches an attack against the Separatist droids.

GENERAL GRIEVOUS
General Grievous is a cyborg who commands the droid army. He hates the Jedi and wants to destroy Obi-Wan.

©2014 LEGO

GENERAL KENOBI
The Jedi General lands on Utapau with a battalion of clone troopers. He is determined not to let General Grievous escape.

©2014 LEGO

©2014 LEGO

MAGNAGUARDS
Grievous surrounds himself with droid bodyguards called MagnaGuards. They are strong, but Obi-Wan defeats them easily.

©2014 LEGO

WHEEL BIKE
Grievous rides a speedy wheel bike. The bike has four clawed legs to climb up the steep cliffs of Utapau.

BOGA

Obi-Wan climbs onto a varactyl beast named Boga and chases Grievous when the general tries to escape on his wheel bike.

©2014 LEGO

©2014 LEGO

COMMANDER CODY

Commander Cody is Obi-Wan's second in command. He leads the 212th Attack Battalion into battle against the droid army.

©2014 LEGO

HAILFIRE DROID

Hailfire droids unleash their many missiles against the clone army. With big wheels and missile launchers, they are a scary sight. Run!

©2014 LEGO

OCTUPTARRA TRI-DROID

This skinny, three-legged droid can turn its head and fire lasers in any direction. It is not easy to destroy this droid.

INVADING FORCE

Droid soldiers patrol the planet Utapau. Can the clone troopers defeat them?

©2014 LEGO

UTAPAU TROOPERS

Troopers from the 212th Attack Battalion wear their orange-marked armour with pride.

15

SIEGE OF SALEUCAMI

The Republic discovers top-secret Separatist cloning factories on the planet Saleucami. Jedi General Stass Allie and her team of clone troopers lead an attack against the factories, but they face tough resistance from the droid army. After a tense battle, the Jedi succeed in their mission.

SALEUCAMI TROOPER

The Republic's 91st Recon Corps patrol Saleucami. Troopers ride BARC speeders to travel over the crater-filled landscape.

STASS ALLIE

Stass Allie is a powerful healer. She prefers negotiation to war, but she knows that the Clone Wars could save the Republic.

STAP

Battle droids ride on Single Trooper Aerial Platforms (STAPs), which are equipped with dual blaster cannons.

SALEUCAMI CANNON

Battle droids hide their cannons in the reeds and shrubs of Saleucami. They wait for the Jedi and clone troopers to speed past.

AMBUSH

Watch out for hidden super battle droids! Their arm blasters are deadly.